This book belongs to

NIKO Dallas

This edition published by Parragon Books Ltd in 2014
and distributed by
Parragon Inc.
440 Park Avenue South, 13th Floor
New York, NY 10016
www.parragon.com

Written by Steve Smallman
Illustrated by Nicola Slater
Edited by Laura Baker
Designed by Ailsa Cullen
Production by Marina Blackburn

ISBN 978-1-4723-5096-1

Printed in China

SPOT A LOT

AND COUNT
A LITTLE, TOO!

ANIMAL ESCAPE

STEVE SMALLMAN   NICOLA SLATER

PARROTS

GIBBONS

GIRAFFE

WARTHOGS

FLAMINGOS

PaRragon

Bath · New York · Cologne · Melbourne · Delhi
Hong Kong · Shenzhen · Singapore · Amsterdam

There's trouble at the zoo today ...

The animals have run away!

GIBBONS

ZEBRAS

FLAMINGOS

TOWN

ZOO

Find and follow the tortoise on every page!

1 very tall giraffe

Spot the little white mouse.

trying hard not to laugh.

Where is the ladybug?

Find 1 green bird.

2 elephants in socks

playing peekaboo in the rocks.

Where is the hippo hiding?

Peekaboo!

Spot 3 green lizards.

3 orange gazelles jumping high—

Find my 4 froggy friends.

they don't need trampolines to fly!

Spot 2 penguins doing backflips.

Spot the soaring dog—and his hat!

swinging by the jungle gym!

Spot the balancing lizard.

Who's in there?

Find the jumping mouse.

5 pretty pink flamingos

Spot the pink umbrella.

posing in the bakery windows!

Find 4 slithering snakes.

6 zebras, white and black,

Spot the dog in a white hat.

going across the
road and back.

Spot 4 mice out and about.

Where's my other shoe?

7 batty little bats
wearing silly party hats.

Find a boot out of place.

Spot 10 pink birds
at the party.

Where is the little bumblebee?

Find the thirsty frog.

8 penguins keeping cool

Where is my pink ball?

splashing at the swimming pool.

Spot 2 bunnies in swim caps.

9 sneaky little parrots hiding by the piles of carrots.

Find 2 frogs at the market stand.

Spot the little orange squirrel.

10 warthogs tapping feet

Spot the snoozing mouse.

Can you find my 2 bunny friends?

dancing to a hip-hop beat!

Find the fox in sunglasses.

Where is my orange bag?

The keeper says,

"Don't make a fuss.
Now, everybody,
on the bus!"

Soon they're back
home in the zoo,

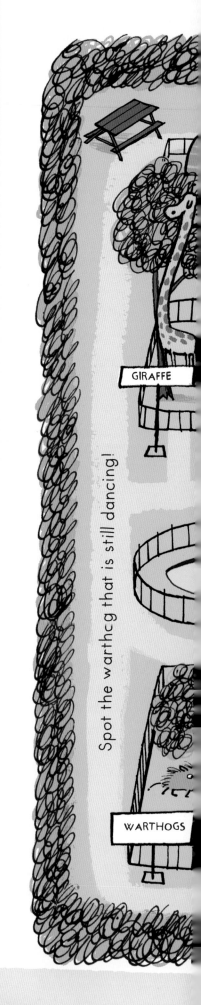

Spot the warthog that is still dancing!

GIRAFFE

WARTHOGS

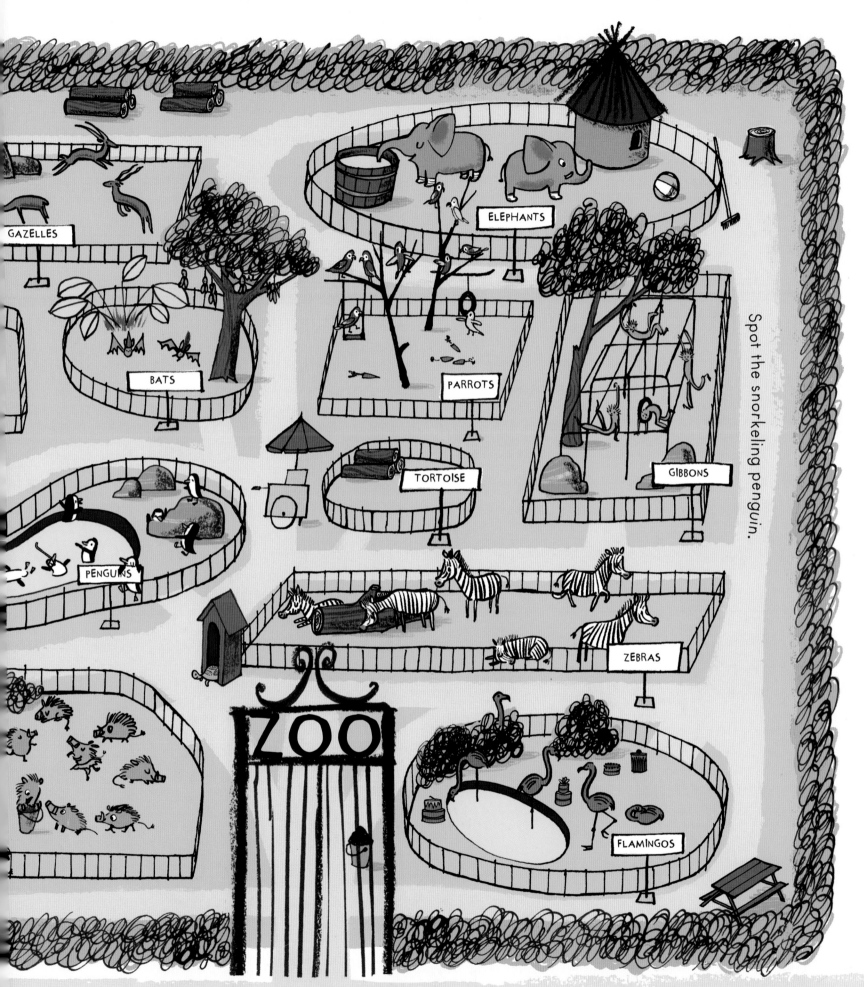

Spot the snorkeling penguin.

but oh no, Tortoise, where are you?

THE END